Angel

by the same author

MONA LISA

DREAM OF A BEAST
(*Chatto & Windus*)

THE PAST
(*Jonathan Cape*)

NIGHT IN TUNISIA AND OTHER STORIES
(*Brandon, Dingle*)

Angel

NEIL JORDAN

faber and faber

LONDON · BOSTON

First published in 1989
by Faber and Faber Limited
3 Queen Square London WC1N 3AU

Photoset and printed in Great Britain by
Redwood Burn Limited, Trowbridge, Wiltshire
All rights reserved

British Library Cataloguing in Publication Data

Jordan, Neil
Angel
I. Title
822'.914   PR6060.06255

ISBN 0-571-14913-8

Contents

Introduction

What is the point of publishing a screenplay? And which version should be published? The script it was intended to shoot, the often radically altered one that was actually shot, or one that reflects the final edited film?

Movie scripts pass through many stages, each one serving a particular purpose. Early scripts are designed to give story editors, producers, financiers, a good read. They must explain everything, and rattle along, for these fellows have notoriously brief attention spans, are often semi-literate and feel threatened by unfamiliar words. Experienced writers/directors omit all camera directions, scene numbers and other technical data at this stage, partly to make smoother reading, but mostly out of recognition that many changes will occur before definitive scene numbers can be assigned and the technical directions will be systematically added by the director as the project develops towards a shooting script. Inexperienced writers often put in numbers and camera directions hoping to impress. It has the reverse effect.

Once a project is financed, a shooting script is the next stage. The accretions of technical detail make this script stodgy and indigestible. It now becomes the equivalent of the handbook in the glove compartment of your car. It should contain as much information as possible for the technicians and actors: day or night, exterior or interior, number of extras, props, clothes, type of shots, descriptions of locations or sets, moods and intentions of the characters.

However carefully a film is prepared, everything changes when you start shooting. If a movie has life, it grows and develops all the time. An actor gives a particularly expressive look which renders a line of dialogue superfluous; a camera movement creates a gap that needs filling with an extra line; a different, more economical way of staging a scene emerges. The more the camera takes over the telling of the story, the further away the film gets from its literary origins. If the movie succeeds in becoming highly cinematic, then the script resembles an attempt to describe a painting or a piece of music.

The next document that emerges is the 'continuity' script. As each scene is filmed, the shots are described and related to the whole. This is a cutting-room guide and a halfway house between script and finished film. To the uninitiated it looks as though a mathematician has been making calculations and inscribing graphics at random over the written pages.

When the film is finally completed, a 'release' script is prepared. The purpose of this is to provide a legal record of what the film actually contains, and as a guide for the preparation of foreign language versions. Someone sits down at an editing machine and describes each scene. It is the script process in exact reverse. When the film is highly cinematic, the release script is an opaque and impenetrable document. It follows that a perfect script of a great film would be totally indecipherable except to the director and his collaborators.

Followers of Jordan's prose writing will detect familiar echoes in the following screenplay, but will also be struck by the dissimilarities. Paradoxically, his short stories are more visual, even more cinematic than this script, which perhaps endorses my theory. These are an architect's drawings. They are fascinating, but hardly prepare us for the finished building. Most interesting is the dialogue which is composed in a style which I call 'poetic cliché'. The characters mostly swap platitudes, but by repetition and rhythm, Jordan stylizes their exchanges. This is not entirely evident on the page as when played at a certain pace and against the tension of realistic staging.

Angel's style and structure (not its story content) were partly inspired by my film *Point Blank* where Alex Jacobs and I attempted a somewhat similar dialogue effect.

I produced *Angel*; that is to say, I organized the finance and practical arrangements, trying to provide Neil with a crew and environment in which he could express his vision, which was entirely his own. It was a Channel 4 film. There was not enough time or money for such an ambitious project by a director making his first film. He had the good fortune to have Chris Menges as his cameraman. Chris was marvellously sensitive to Neil's needs and would always present to him the camera choices available in each set-up without influencing him towards his own preferences. Walter Donohue, then of Channel 4, supported him in other subtle ways and we all had the satisfaction of witnessing the tortured struggles and triumphant emergence of a film artist.

JOHN BOORMAN

Angel was first shown on 4 November 1982 at the Scala Cinema and the Paris Pullman in London.

The cast was as follows:

ANNIE	Veronica Quilligan
DANNY	Stephen Rea
BILL	Alan Devlin
RAY	Peter Caffrey
DEIRDRE	Honor Heffernan
BRIDE	Lisa-Ann McLaughlin
BRIDEGROOM	Ian McElhinney
BEST MAN	Derek Lord
BLOOM	Ray McAnally
BONNER	Donal McCann
AUNT MAE	Marie Kean
BOUNCER	Don Foley
ASSISTANT	Gerald McSorley
GEORGE	Tony Rohr
BETH	Anita Reeves
MARY	Sorcha Cusack
MAN	Michael Lally
FRANCIE	Macrea Clarke

Director	Neil Jordan
Executive Producer	John Boorman
Producer	Barry Blackmore
Photography	Chris Menges
Art Director	John Lucas
Music	Paddy Meegan
Saxophone solos	Keith Donald

1. EVENING. EXT. DANCE HALL

A plain brick dance hall set in a tarmac square among empty fields.
There is a sign over the main doorway reading Dreamland. ANNIE
leans against the brick wall, her cheek against the concrete, looking
towards the van which is parked on the tarmac. She has blonde hair,
ill-fitting clothes and a strangely simple-minded, sensuous face.
There are bursts of saxophone music coming from the van, drifting
across the fields beyond.
BILL *gets out of the van and moves into the dance hall.*
Inside the van DANNY *is perched on his sax case, his eyes closed, his*
cheeks against the metal wall. He is wearing a red showband suit.
He is improvising lazily on the saxophone, as if testing its tone. The
cascade of notes falls into the melody 'Danny Boy', then returns to
random scales.
ANNIE *walks slowly along the wall of the dance hall. She keeps one*
palm pressed against the brick like a child. She turns with the angle
of the wall and comes to a doorway. She leans against the doorway,
looking towards the van.
BILL, *the band's drummer, comes from the dance hall interior. He is*
a large, burly man. He finds ANNIE *blocking his way. He stops for*
a moment, as if unwilling to pass. Then she steps suddenly aside, as
if sensing him behind her. She watches him pass by her. She catches
his eye and gives a slight smile.
BILL: (*Goes to the van and climbs inside*) You've got an audience.
  (*Picks up drum.*)
  (DANNY *doesn't answer.*)
  Give her the Soldier's Song.
  (DANNY *plays on.* BILL *carries the drum back, passes* ANNIE
  again and moves into the darkness of the hall.
  DANNY's *playing peters out. He shakes the drops from his sax*
  and rises, taking the case in one hand and the sax in the other.
  He steps out of the van and walks towards the hall. ANNIE
  smiles as he approaches. DANNY *stops in front of her.*)

I

DANNY: (*Puts top on sax and jumps down from van*) What's your
name?
(*Her lips flicker uncertainly. She reaches out a hand and
touches his sax.*)
It's a saxophone.
(*She pulls her hand away, turning her head away at the same
time.* DANNY *walks past her into the hall.*)

2. EVENING. INT. DANCE HALL
DANNY *walks down a dim corridor into the hall. The band are on
the bandstand at the other end, connecting their mikes and
instruments.* RAY, *the band's manager, is standing in the centre of
the floor.*
RAY: Come on lads, it's not the bloody Halle Orchestra – Van
Morrison eat your heart out. Here he comes, boys. The
Stan Getz of South Armagh.
DANNY: Who's the girl?
RAY: What girl?

(DANNY *points back towards the corridor, through which*
ANNIE *can be seen framed in the doorway*.)
She comes with the hall.
(DANNY *moves towards the stage*.)
DANNY: (*Looking round the hall*) Were we here before?
RAY: (*Off-shot*) Aye, and they liked us too. We got a bigger
crowd than Dickie Rock.
BILL: (*Shouting from the stage*): Are they paying danger money?
RAY: None of that, boys. We're musicians. Music hath
charms . . .
DANNY: You developing a lisp? Where's the bandroom in this kip?
BILL: It's in the back. Tell Di to make it snappy.

3. EVENING. INT. DRESSING-ROOM
DEIRDRE, *the band's singer, is sitting in front of a cracked mirror,*
making up. She is in a gold dress, half zipped at the back.
DANNY: (*In doorway*) I think he's developing a lisp.
DEIRDRE: Who is?
DANNY: Your man.
(DANNY *enters. He crosses to the sink, wets his hair, then*
moves to the mirror, looking straight at her. She does her best to
ignore him.)
(*Combing his hair*) A bit more around the eyes.
DEIRDRE: Give over.
DANNY: That's nice.
DEIRDRE: I have to look good. Keep you boys in business.
DANNY: (*Puts spray down*) You always do.
(*He touches her neck.*) Will you be around later?
DEIRDRE: Ask my manager.
DANNY: Fuck your manager.
DEIRDRE: Aye, maybe I will.
DANNY: Don't.
(*He touches her neck again.*)
DEIRDRE: Give over, would you, and zip me up.
(*He zips her up. Kisses her neck.*)
DANNY: See you later.
(*He exits.* DEIRDRE *laughs.*)

3

4. NIGHT. EXT. DANCE HALL

The tarmac square is dark by now. A series of bright headlights wheel into and around it. Groups of men and women get out of cars, some drunk, some laughing.

DANNY emerges from the hall. He passes ANNIE again at the doorway, where there is a ticket desk, and goes to the van. Lying on the floor of the van is the pull-through to his saxophone – a piece of chamois tied by a string to a small metal ball. He picks it up and walks back towards the hall. The ticket desk has been set up in the doorway and there is a line of people moving towards it. ANNIE is still there, leaning against the door, watching the crowd go through.

DANNY: (*Goes up to* ANNIE) Are you not coming in? This is a pull-through. Come on.

    (*To* BOUNCER) She's with me.

BOUNCER: Rules of the hall. No passes.

DANNY: I love you.

    (DANNY *takes a note and throws it in the till.*) Two pounds.

    (*To* BOUNCER) Now are you happy?

BOUNCER: She's not worth half that, are you, Annie?

    (DANNY *enters the hall followed by* ANNIE.)

5. NIGHT. INT. DANCE HALL

The band strikes up, playing 'Blood is Thicker than Water'.

DANNY: Will we dance?

    (*He takes* ANNIE *in his arms and dances her into the empty hall.* DEIRDRE *is singing from the stage.*)

    Do you come here often? (*He looks closely at her.*) Aye, you do, don't you?

    (ANNIE *dances clumsily, smiling at him.*)

    You shouldn't smile that much. You'll set people thinking . . .

    (*The song peters to a halt after a bar or two.* RAY *walks over to* DANNY *across the empty floor.*)

RAY: Time you were on stage.

    (DANNY *slips* ANNIE's *arm on to* RAY.)

DANNY: You look after her now.

    (DANNY *walks towards the stage. As he does so,* DEIRDRE *takes up the song again. The hall slowly fills up with people.*

4

RAY *begins to dance with* ANNIE.)

RAY: Let's show them, sunshine.

(RAY *sweeps her in elaborate turns round the floor. He is a very good dancer.*)

Someone has to show them. Stop them holding up the walls.

(DEIRDRE *comes to the end of a verse and* DANNY *goes into a soaring solo on the sax. Other couples take to the floor.*)

He's good, isn't he? That good he's ridiculous. (*He glances towards the alcove.*) I'll have to leave you sunshine. I've got things to do.

(*She keeps dancing.* RAY *stops her by the elbow.*)

I said I've got things to do . . .

(*She stands still.*)

That's better.

(*He walks towards the alcove, leaving* ANNIE *in the centre of the floor. She looks off at* RAY *then turns to watch* DANNY.)

6. NIGHT. EXT. DANCE HALL

Two cars drive on to the tarmac: the first a wedding car with the bride and groom and best man, the second with the bridesmaids and wedding guests.

They get out of the cars and move to the entrance.

BRIDE: You call this a honeymoon?

BEST MAN: He does – he calls it a honeymoon.

BRIDE: Leave him be. My John is sentimental. This is where he picked me up.

> (*They move into the ballroom.*)

7. NIGHT. INT. BANDSTAND

DANNY *shakes the drops from his sax after the number.* DEIRDRE *turns to him.*

DEIRDRE: You love that thing, don't you?

DANNY: Aye, but am I any good?

DEIRDRE: You're not bad . . .

> (DANNY *looks downstage, where* ANNIE *is moving across the empty floor.*)

6

8. NIGHT. INT. DANCE HALL

The hall is now crammed. The band is in the middle of a song. The crowd sways back and forwards like one single body, lost in the music. ANNIE *stands by the wall, swaying back and forwards in imitation of the crowd, but out of time with the music. The* BRIDE *pushes her way through the mass of people like a white bird, with her entourage behind her. She dances with her sullen groom,* JOHN, *who is very drunk.*

BRIDE: Hey, let's dance.

JOHN: You know I can't dance.

BRIDE: Come on. It's our wedding day.

    (ANNIE *comes forward. Stares at* DANNY.)

9. NIGHT. EXT. DANCE HALL

RAY *throws a youth bodily out of the dance hall and roughs him up.*

RAY: You get the fuck out. Little shit. You stay away from me and my band. Do you hear me? You just go and sing for your money. I'm protected already. I'm warning you, don't come here again, otherwise you'll find yourself missing a kneecap.

    (*He throws him into the arms of a second man – they go.* RAY *returns to the hall.*)

10. NIGHT. INT. BANDSTAND

DANNY *is sitting at the edge of the stage, while the band play above him. He is dreaming, listening to the music. The* BRIDE *sidles up to him.*

BRIDE: Why aren't you up there?

DANNY: They don't need me for this.

BRIDE: Didn't you used to play with the Las Vegas?

    (DANNY *shakes his head.*)

    They had a saxman just like you.

DANNY: We all look the same.

BRIDE: Going to ask me to dance?

DANNY: Will you dance?

    (*He looks up and sees the groom some way off.*)

BRIDE: I can't. I'm married.

7

(DANNY *stands and moves up on the stage. The groom,* JOHN, *moves towards the* BRIDE.)

JOHN: What are you doing talking to him for, for fuck's sake?

BRIDE: Nothing. Come on.

(*They vanish into the crowd.*)

11. NIGHT. EXT. DANCE HALL

Crowds are emerging from the hall. There is the sound of the National Anthem being played on sax from inside. The BOUNCER *leans against a car, predatory in the moonlight.*

12. NIGHT. INT. DRESSING-ROOM

DANNY *is sitting in front of the mirror as before. He cleans each piece of his sax and puts it into the felt-lined case. He hears a noise outside the window.*

DANNY: Di?

(*He moves to the window. The figure vanishes into the darkness. He opens the door and follows it.*)

8

13. NIGHT. EXT. DANCE HALL

Out on the tarmac, DANNY *moves towards the hall across the tarmac shouting Deirdre's name. He receives no reply. He peers into the darkness of the fields. There is a large tree there with lights. He walks towards the tree. When he reaches it, he stands for a moment, looking at the moon, listening. He can hear nothing. Then a pair of female hands cover his eyes from behind. He grips them with his own hands. The hands pull him down on to the grass.*

DANNY: So you asked your manager?

(*He pulls the girl in front of him and realizes it is* ANNIE, *not Deirdre. He pulls away suddenly.*)

Sorry. I thought you were her.

(ANNIE *gazes at him with the intensity of a child.*)

Her who sings . . .

(ANNIE *pulls at the sax band around his neck.*)

You're too young . . .

(*They lie beneath the tree.*)

14. NIGHT. EXT. DANCE HALL

The van is fully loaded. DEIRDRE *comes from the hall.* RAY *follows her out.*

DEIRDRE: (*Calling*) Danny –

RAY: Do you really like him that much?

DEIRDRE: Where the hell is he?

RAY: You go on with Bill. I'll take him.
> (*She kisses him.*)

DEIRDRE: And tell him where to put it too –
> (*She walks across to the van and climbs in. It drives off, past* RAY, *who stands there waiting for* DANNY.)

15. NIGHT. EXT. TREE

DANNY: That's a wishing tree.
> (ANNIE's *hand reaches up and takes a bell from the tree.* RAY *moves inside the dance hall.* DANNY *moves from the tree towards some abandoned construction pipes.* ANNIE *is there.* DANNY *climbs in and kisses her.*)

16. NIGHT. INT. DANCE HALL

RAY *stands behind the bar in the dance hall counting money.*

17. NIGHT. EXT. PIPES

ANNIE *puts the bell on to his sax neckpiece and moves away from him.*

DANNY: Are you all right?
> (ANNIE *moves away.*)
> Is this what they taught you in convent school? You can't hear me, can you? You're beautiful. (*He turns his head away from her.*) Did you hear that?
> (*Suddenly two cars screech on to the tarmac and stop outside the ballroom door.* ANNIE *moves forward to stand on the edge of the tarmac.* DANNY *stares after her. Two men get out of the red car and move into the ballroom.*
> *Men bundle* RAY *outside the ballroom door.*)

RAY: Blow the hall if you like lads, but leave me be –

MAN: You were making payments –

RAY: I was told to –

11

MAN: Tell this to someone.
  (*He shoots* RAY *in the stomach.*)
  He's been a bad boy.
  (MAN *shoots* RAY *in the side of the head.* DANNY, *still in the pipes, looks on, horrified. He sees a man with a club foot nudge* RAY's *body with his surgical boot.*
  ANNIE *sees the body of* RAY. *The men see* ANNIE.)
MAN: Who the fuck is she?
OTHER MAN: It doesn't matter who she is, John.
  (*There is a burst of fire from* JOHN's *gun.* ANNIE's *body is jerked backwards towards the edge of the tarmac, torn apart by the bullets. She falls. The men quickly get into cars and drive off.*
  DANNY *moves from the pipes to* ANNIE. *He picks her up in his arms.*)
DANNY: Why didn't you stay! Come on, come on. I'll help you.
  (*The ballroom explodes. Fire rushes from the windows and the foyer.* DANNY *and* ANNIE *are blown backwards.*)

18. THE NEXT MORNING. EXT. PIPES

DANNY, *holding* ANNIE *on his lap, is found seated against the pipes.*

DANNY: I'll teach you to sing.

    (*The* RUC *and* UDR *are on the tarmac outside the ballroom –* BONNER *stands outside the burnt-out foyer and is joined by* BLOOM, *who comes from inside.*

    DANNY, *carrying* ANNIE, *moves from behind the pipes towards the ballroom as* BLOOM *and* BONNER *walk down to them.*

    BLOOM *looks at the body of* ANNIE.)

BLOOM: Jesus Christ.

    (DANNY *staggers forward towards the ballroom.*)

19. NIGHT. EXT. DANCE HALL

A shot of the club-footed man walking around RAY's *body.*

20. MORNING. INT. HOSPITAL

With a start, DANNY *opens his eyes and suddenly sits up. He is on a hospital examination table. Cut to the surgical boot nudging* RAY's *body.*

21. MORNING. INT. EXAMINATION ROOM

DANNY *is lying on the examination table.* BLOOM *stands leaning against the wall.* BONNER *stands beside him holding photographs.*

BLOOM: It's so quiet now out there you'd think it was . . .

BONNER: What?

BLOOM: Paradise . . .

    (DANNY *looks up at* BLOOM *at that word.*)

DANNY: What do you know, Mr Bloom?

BLOOM: (*Shrugging*) I know no more than you.

DANNY: You're supposed to ask me questions.

BLOOM: (*Moving to the window*) Did he ever discuss his business with you?

DANNY: Just music.

BLOOM: Why did he stay behind?

DANNY: (*Moves back*) I suppose he was waiting for me.

BLOOM: Did he recognize them?

DANNY: I don't remember.

    (BLOOM *looks at* DANNY. *After a pause,* BONNER *walks towards him, holding photographs.*)

13

BONNER: Have a look at these. (*He gives them to* DANNY.) Just say whatever comes into your mind. Anything at all.
(DANNY *glances through photo after photo, all of men in everyday situations.*)
BLOOM: No one saw you, Danny. You've nothing to be afraid of. Remember that.
DANNY: I saw feet. (*Drops photographs.*) Have you pictures of feet?
(*The photographs remain on the floor at* BLOOM's *and* BONNER's *feet.*)

22. DAY. INT. HOSPITAL CORRIDOR
DANNY *comes out of the ward. The* ORDERLY *is some distance off. He has a brace on one foot.*
DANNY: Hey you.
(*The* ORDERLY *stops and turns towards him.*)
Where did you get your shoes?
(*The* ORDERLY *turns again, without replying. A* GIRL *moves forward to* DANNY. DANNY *is crying.*)

23. DAY. INT. HOSPITAL BEDROOM
DANNY *is standing by the window. His arm is bandaged.* DEIRDRE *enters. She has flowers in her hand.*
DANNY: What's it like out there?
DEIRDRE: Haven't you been out yet?
(DANNY *shakes his head. She gives him flowers.*)
The day of the funeral was like Heaven. You could see the mountains. What happened, Danny? Won't you tell me?
(DANNY *doesn't answer.*)
Don't you remember?
(DEIRDRE *begins to smile, as if to stop herself crying.*)
He had the whole band insured. Like he expected something. Bill's got a hall down Bull Alley. He's bought a Mercedes van. He's going to manage us. Or he's going to try. He's got your sax there, waiting.
(*She crosses to the window and turns. She looks straight at him.*)
He wants you back, Danny. Can he have you?

14

DANNY: Where were you, Di? I was calling you. I wanted to do
this to you –
(*He puts his hands on her face.*)
Then I did it to someone else.

24. DAY. EXT. HIGH BUILDING
DANNY *walks along the street towards a high-rise building. There is
broken glass everywhere and none of the flats seem inhabited. At the
far end there is a woman hanging out washing on a line between the
flat door and the balcony wall.* DANNY *calls* AUNTIE MAE. *She
turns and moves to the railings.*
DANNY: (*Throws down bag*) Hello Mae.
MAE: Where have you been?
DANNY: I was touring.
MAE: You always are.
DANNY: Put on the kettle, Mae.
(*They enter the flat.*)

25. DAY. INT. MAE'S FLAT
*The flat is surrounded with an extraordinary array of knick-knacks –
a bit like a fairground or a fortune-teller's caravan. There is a
photograph on the mantelpiece, of a man in a dress suit, with a
saxophone, surrounded by an old-style dance band.*
MAE: Why have none of our breed got sense? Always chasing
glitter. Music, lights, anything that glitters. May as well
chase shadows – (*Takes cigarette and lights it.*)
DANNY: (*Moves to her*) It's got charms, Mae.
MAE: Who told you that one?
DANNY: He did. (*He nods towards the man in the photograph.*)
(MAE *looks at it. The man in the photograph seems to smile at
her.*)
MAE: Where did it get him?
DANNY: It got him you.
MAE: I'll get you a cup of tea.
(*She exits.* DANNY *looks at the photograph.*)

26. NIGHT. INT. MAE'S FLAT

DANNY *and* MAE *sit at the table.* MAE *holds the cards. She places the Jack of Clubs on the table.*

MAE: I remember you playing in the bandstand in Portstewart. Him and me looking on, as proud as punch. The wind whipping round your wee ankles. (*Hands pack to* DANNY.) (DANNY *cuts the cards.*)

DANNY: A dark lady and a government man . . .

MAE: I used to read them round here till it got too uncomfortable. (MAE *picks up the cards.*) They kept turning up black. (*She starts to place the cards on the table.*) Who wants to pay to see the Ace of Spades?

DANNY: Am I going to cross water, Mae?

MAE: When the last day comes, I'd think, every one'll turn up black. All over this city, thousands and thousands of Aces of Spades. (*She places an eight, then Ace on the Jack.*) At the same day, the same hour. And we'll know it not . . . (*She turns up the Ace of Spades. She picks up the four cards.*)

DANNY: What do they say?

MAE: (*She gathers up the rest of the cards.*) I've lost the knack, son. You play us a tune.

DANNY: I've lost my saxophone.

MAE: We've all lost something.

27. NIGHT. INT. INNER ROOM, MAE'S FLAT

MAE, *followed by* DANNY, *moves through the living-room to the bedroom. She opens the door and switches on the light.*

MAE: You'll remember him in here. Good-night, flower.

DANNY: Good-night, Mae.

(MAE *leaves.* DANNY *closes the door. He moves around the bedroom, starts to take off his shirt. Takes off his watch and places it beside the bed – picks up a metronome. It starts to tick.* DANNY *looks at his uncle's photograph pinned on the wall.*)

28. DAY. INT./EXT. FLAT
DANNY *wakes up in the flat in the morning. It is a bright,*
wonderful day. DANNY *sits upright on the bed. His heels bang*
against something under the bed. He pulls it out. It is a small
instrument case. He opens it and finds a small silver soprano sax. He
begins to play it. He moves to the window, looking downwards.
Outside a middle-aged woman carrying a shopping basket walks
across the street passing a soldier with a rifle, his back against the
wall. DANNY *takes the saxophone from his mouth, and stares. A*
series of flashbacks of the night of the Dance Hall murders begins.

29. DAY. INT. CINEMA
The band are in rehearsal.
BILL: Could you accent that a bit more? It was a bit quiet that
   time. Right – after four.
   (DANNY *moves into the doorway of the darkened theatre.*)
DEIRDRE: (*Singing*)
   'Looking at you you're not the same any more.
   What can I do, to stop you going through that door . . .
   Blood is thicker than . . .'
   (*She stops singing.*)
BILL: Di . . .
DEIRDRE: There's somebody down there.
BILL: For Christ's sake.
   (DEIRDRE *moves forward to meet* DANNY *moving up on to the*
   stage.)
DEIRDRE: Oh, it's you.
DANNY: You told me to come.
BILL: We did that.
DANNY: (*Crossing the stage*) I'm here. (*Throws overcoat on to*
   amplifier. He walks up on to the stage. There is a moment of
   slight nervousness.)
BILL: The lads were superstitious. They wouldn't come back.
   (DANNY *stares at the two new members.*)
   We couldn't do without you though.
DANNY: No?
BILL: (*Throws the neckpiece at him*) We held on to your sax.
   (BILL *hands the saxophone to* DANNY.)

17

I suppose you were wondering about it.

(DANNY *looks down at his sax.*)

DANNY: No . . . (*He hooks the saxophone on to the neckpiece.*)
I've forgotten how.

BILL: Don't give us that, Danny. You couldn't forget.

DANNY: It's my hand. (*Takes top off sax.*)

BILL: Let's try 'Thicker than Water', just like before.

(DANNY *nods, moves forward, blowing sax.*)

DANNY: Do I make you nervous?

BILL: (*Off-shot*) Don't worry about it, Danny, you'll get it back.

DANNY: The Stan Getz of South Armagh . . .

(BILL *beats out time on the drum.* DEIRDRE *starts to sing.*)

DEIRDRE: 'Blood is thicker than water, baby, and
deeper than wine. You've had a change of heart,
I wish that somebody'd change mine.'

(DANNY *continues with a sax solo.*)

30. DAY. INT. BACKSTAGE DRESSING-ROOM

DANNY *sits on a chair cleaning his sax. Around him are posters and pictures of movie stars.*

DEIRDRE *moves in and leans in the doorway.*

DEIRDRE: Why did you come in like that?

DANNY: Like what?

(DEIRDRE *moves into the room.*)

DEIRDRE: Like a ghost.

DANNY: I just came in.

DEIRDRE: The Stan Getz of South Armagh. (*She kisses him.*) You're still good, you know.

31. DAY. EXT. ORTHOPAEDIC SHOP

DANNY, *carrying his sax case, walks along the street, stops, and looks into the window. He sees orthopaedic shoes.*

32. DAY. EXT. GRAVEYARD

DANNY *and* MAE *are walking through the graveyard. There is a wind blowing through it.* MAE *is holding flowers.*

MAE: There was magic in you. That's what he'd tell me. When you played, there was a halo round you.

DANNY: I found his soprano.

MAE: No need for cards here. I can hear him. And all the dead voices.

(*The wind blows around them.* MAE *lays flowers on a grave.* DANNY *stares around at the hundreds of gravestones.*)

I used to pray until he died. Then I didn't need to.

(*She turns to* DANNY.)

DANNY: Can you see things, Mae?

MAE: Something's happened, hasn't it? A woman.

DANNY: Look –

(BLOOM *is standing some distance off, a car behind him.*)

Are you looking for me?

BLOOM: Yes, I was. You left the hospital without telling us. And we do have to know where you are.

DANNY: Why?

BLOOM: All sorts of reasons. You might remember –

DANNY: But I won't.

19

BLOOM: Maybe you will. Where do you live?

DANNY: With my Auntie Mae.

BLOOM: And what's your address?

DANNY: 57 Bellevue Buildings.

BLOOM: Call in in a few days. Coleraine Street. Ask for me.
(*He gets into the car and drives off.*)

MAE: He's the government man.
(*They walk through the graveyard.*)
What is it, Danny?

DANNY: A girl.

MAE: Where is she?

DANNY: She's dead.

33. DAY. EXT. ORTHOPAEDIC SHOP

DANNY, *carrying his sax case, walks along the street, stops and looks into window.*

34. DAY. INT. DRESSING-ROOM

DANNY *and* DEIRDRE *are sitting in the dressing-room.* BILL *enters.*

BILL: What we need is a bit of glitter – new suits, nice jackets, straight lapels right down to here – maybe a gold clasp – long jackets, a black and silver stripe down the leg – and a flare – an insert flare. What colour do you think? (*He takes a puff of a cigarette.*)

DANNY: Pink.

BILL: Why pink?

DANNY: It's a nice colour.

BILL: What do you think?

DEIRDRE: It's nice.

BILL: (*Leaving*) Yeah – I suppose pink.
(*He goes.*)

DEIRDRE: Give him a chance.

DANNY: That's what I'm doing. (*He rises and looks at a photograph.*)
(DEIRDRE *rises at the same time.*)
(*Pointing to photograph*) Who's that?

DEIRDRE: Monica Vitti.

DANNY: Who's Monica Vitti?
DEIRDRE: What is it, Danny?
DANNY: It's a dream.
DEIRDRE: What's a dream?
DANNY: Pink – (*He touches her on the lip.*)

35. DAY. EXT. STREETS. ORTHOPAEDIC SHOP
DANNY *walks down the street. He comes to the same shop. He stops again and looks at the display of black shining leather boots, all with enlarged heels.*

36. DAY. INT. SHOP
DANNY *enters the shop and looks at the various boxes on the shelves. He picks up an enlarged shoe on the counter. The* ASSISTANT *is looking at him.*
ASSISTANT: Can I help you?
DANNY: I'm looking for shoes.
ASSISTANT: This is a specialist shop.
DANNY: Aye. You specialize in shoes.
ASSISTANT: We only deal with prescribed patients.
DANNY: So how does a body buy your shoes?
ASSISTANT: You get a prescription. Try the Royal Hospital.
DANNY: I've been there.
   (GIRL ASSISTANT *enters from the right.*)
GIRL ASSISTANT: You're wanted on the phone.
ASSISTANT: Excuse me –
   (*The* ASSISTANT *moves away along the corridor to answer the phone.* DANNY *reacts to the fact that the* ASSISTANT *wears a surgical boot.*)
   (*On the phone*) Look, I told you not to call me here.
   (DANNY *is mesmerized by the* ASSISTANT'*s feet.*)
GIRL ASSISTANT: Is there anything you want? We're closing for
   lunch.
   (DANNY *turns away and moves towards the door. He finds it closed. The male* ASSISTANT *moves to the door.*)
ASSISTANT: Like I said, try the Royal –
DANNY: Thank you.
   (*The* ASSISTANT *unlocks the door for him –* DANNY *exits.*)

21

37. DAY. EXT. STREET

DANNY *stands in front of a florist's shop. The* ASSISTANT *emerges from the shop. He walks with a slight limp. He walks down the street. He passes* DANNY. DANNY *follows him.*

The ASSISTANT *turns another corner and comes to a row of houses. He opens the door of one of them and enters.*

DANNY *follows at a distance – he looks through the window and sees the* ASSISTANT *making preparations for a meal.*

DANNY *moves on down the street, ducks beneath a wire, crosses a piece of waste ground and moves to the back of the house.*

38. DAY. EXT. BACK DOOR

He looks through the window of the back door. He is in time to see the ASSISTANT *move from his living-room.*

DANNY *ducks away from the door. The* ASSISTANT *leaves the house.*

DANNY *pulls up the window of the bathroom, which rises easily. He climbs inside.*

39. DAY. INT. FLAT

DANNY *moves from the bathroom along the corridor and into the living-room. He begins to search the room, gradually becoming more angry. He throws the coats and magazines on to the floor, rips the posters from the wall, pulls out drawers and upsets the contents. He takes clothes and shoes from the cupboard and throws them around the room. He picks up a box and throws it down – it falls open and reveals the parts of a gun. He picks up the parts and stands.*

He starts to assemble the gun. He cocks the gun.

He hears the front door opening. DANNY *stares at the door. It opens and the* ASSISTANT *stands there, with a jar of honey in his hand. He is too surprised to speak.*

They stare at each other for a moment. There is a strange sense of recognition in their eyes.

DANNY: I wanted to talk to you. What's your name?

 (*The* ASSISTANT *quickly shuts the door.*

 DANNY *fires a single shot, then four shots in quick succession – he looks horrified at what he has done.*

22

DANNY *moves to the door and opens it. The* ASSISTANT *falls into the room on to his back. He is covered in blood and honey.* DANNY *moves over to him – he places the gun beside him.*)
I wanted to tell you how beautiful she was.

40. DAY. INT. CINEMA
The band is playing. DEIRDRE *is singing 'Strange Fruit'.*
DEIRDRE: 'Here is fruit for the crows to pluck...'
    (*Camera pans left to pick up* DANNY *playing a sax solo.*)

41. DAY. EXT. CINEMA
DANNY *and* DEIRDRE *are outside the cinema. They cross the street.*
DEIRDRE: You sounded great in there.
DANNY: Did I?
DEIRDRE: We're going to play your tune.
DANNY: What tune?
DEIRDRE: 'Danny Boy'. For the slow set.
DANNY: That's not my tune. That's everybody's.
    (*They walk towards* DEIRDRE'S *car.*)
DEIRDRE: It'll be all right, you know. Someone's looking after you.
DANNY: Tell me who –
DEIRDRE: I can see it when you play. You're charmed...
    (DEIRDRE *throws the keys of the car to* DANNY. DANNY *unlocks the car – gets in – unlocks the passenger door.* DEIRDRE *gets in. They drive away.*)

42. DAY. INT. DRIVING CAR
DANNY *is driving. The car comes to a stop near the assistant's flat.*
DEIRDRE: This isn't my way.
    (DANNY *stops the engine. The canal is to their left.*)
DANNY: I know. Can we stop for a bit?
    (*They sit in silence for a moment.*)
DEIRDRE: I meant that, you know. There's a spell on you.
DANNY: Now you tell me –
DEIRDRE: Didn't notice it before. But maybe I didn't look.
    (*She notices* DANNY'S *silence.*)

Am I talking too much?
(DANNY *looks through his rear-view mirror. He can see the*
window of the assistant's flat.)
DANNY: No, you're not.
DEIRDRE: You say something for a change.
(DANNY *keeps his eye on the mirror.*)
DANNY: 'Shall I compare thee to a summer's day?'
DEIRDRE: How nice.
(DANNY *suddenly turns to her.*)
DANNY: Can I touch your hair?
(*He touches her hair. His eyes flicker back to the mirror.*)
DEIRDRE: Why don't you look at me?
DANNY: (*Looks at her*) Can I kiss you?
(DEIRDRE *nods.* DANNY *kisses her on the mouth. She closes*
her eyes. His eyes flicker again towards the mirror. DEIRDRE's
mouth comes away from his.)
DEIRDRE: 'Thou art more lovely and more temperate.'
DANNY: So you were a convent girl?
DEIRDRE: Yes.
(DANNY *looks again at the window of the assistant's flat in the*
rear-view mirror.)
DANNY: Is it time to go?
DEIRDRE: Maybe.
(*He starts the car and drives off.*)

43. NIGHT. INT. ASSISTANT'S FLAT
DANNY *raises the window and climbs inside. The flat is just as*
when he left it. The ASSISTANT's *body is lying on the floor. The*
honey and blood have spilt down his sides and numerous flies are
stuck to it. The gun is there where he left it. He picks it up and cocks
it. There is the sound of the front door opening then, and of footsteps
entering. He hears voices. DANNY *moves behind the door.*
MAN II: Why didn't he answer?
(MAN I *moves into the doorway.*)
MAN I: Jesus wept – (*Moves to body.*)
(MAN II *moves along corridor.*)
MAN II: He's sleeping. Let him sleep.
(*He lights a cigarette.* MAN I *bends down and touches the*

24

honey on the ASSISTANT's *body.*)

MAN I: Honey.

MAN II: He always liked honey.

Come on – (*He turns to go.*)

(DANNY *listens to both of them walk back towards the front door. He turns off the light and exits.*)

44. DAY. INT. MAE'S FLAT

MAE *sits with cards.* DANNY *stands behind her, filling a kettle at the tap.* MAE *is looking at the cards.*

MAE: When Ben was on his uppers, Mae'd read the cards. No gigs coming in, so Mae'd read the cards. Fortunes on the promenade. A dark lady and a government man . . . (*She raises her head.*) Old Nobodaddy walks through them.

DANNY: Who's Nobodaddy?

MAE: He's in the pack. He's got no face. Somewhere between all the other faces. I never know what he looks like. Just know when he's there. I tell lies when I feel him. I say there'll be a wedding, you'll cross water. I tell them anything but him. You don't have to pay to see him.

45. DAY. EXT. STREET

DANNY *walks along the street with his saxophone case. A car comes alongside him and stops.* BLOOM *is in it, accompanied by* BONNER.

BLOOM: Well, Danny? Playing again?

(*Opens door and gets out of car.*)

DANNY: A little.

BLOOM: You were supposed to come and see us. Did you forget?

DANNY: I must have.

BLOOM: You've a bad memory, Danny.

DANNY: I know.

BLOOM: Will you take a lift?

(BONNER *opens back door of car.* BLOOM *gets back inside car.* DANNY *gets in. The car drives away.*)

46. DAY. INT. RUC STATION

BLOOM *followed by* DANNY *followed by* BONNER *enter the*

25

office – BLOOM *crosses over to the hat stand and puts his hat and coat on it.* BONNER *takes the saxophone case from* DANNY.
BONNER: Will I take that for you?
> (*He puts the saxophone case on top of the filing cabinet.* BLOOM *moves to the filing cabinet and takes out a pile of files.*)
BLOOM: Right.
> (*He moves into the inner office.* DANNY *follows.* BLOOM *closes the door.*)

47. DAY. INT. INNER OFFICE
BLOOM *leaning on the window,* DANNY *sitting at the desk with the files in front of him. He looks through the files as* BLOOM *speaks. Each file has a small card with details attached to it and a photograph of the person.*
BLOOM: We could show you every face in the country if it would help you – Catholic, Protestant. By the way, in case you're wondering, I'm Jewish.
DANNY: Are you a Catholic Jew or a Protestant Jew? (*Puts file aside.*) They can't all have done something?
BLOOM: But they can. That's the beauty of it. Every last one of them. Nowadays everybody's guilty.
> (DANNY *comes to a photograph of the man he saw in the assistant's flat. He stares at it, and the card attached. There is a number and an address with the words Dune Cottage somewhere on it.* BLOOM *looks out of the plate glass window, meditative as before.* DANNY *passes on to other photos.*)
BLOOM: Y'see, maybe you're better off forgetting.
DANNY: You asked me to remember.
BLOOM: I know, but it's deep, Danny. It's everywhere and nowhere.
DANNY: What is?
BLOOM: (*As if to himself*) Evil.

48. DUSK. INT. BEDROOM
DANNY *is sitting on the floor of the bedroom – he has the case of his uncle's saxophone on his knee. He takes the saxophone from the case and empties it. He picks up the gun and dismantles it and places it in*

the case. He closes the case and puts it beside him on the floor. He
rises to look out of the window. A car is burning in the street.

49. DAY. EXT. DUNE COTTAGE
Exterior shot of the cottage.

50. DAY. INT. DUNE COTTAGE
There is a photograph on the wall of a woman holding children.
DANNY *is looking at the photograph. He moves round the room,*
pulling aside a curtain and looking into another room. He moves to
the breadbin and helps himself to a slice of bread. He then moves
into the bedroom and sits on the bed. He starts to eat the bread when
he sees the man through the bedroom window approaching the house.
He starts to take the gun from beneath his coat.

51. DAY. INT. DUNE COTTAGE
The man, whistling, enters through the front door, puts his bucket
into the sink and moves to the other room. DANNY *comes out of the*
bedroom and when the man moves to the living-room DANNY *is*
waiting for him with the gun in his hand. The man moves to DANNY
who presses the gun into his stomach.
DANNY: What's over there?
GEORGE: There's the sea.
DANNY: Would you take me to it?
　　(*The man moves to the door followed by* DANNY *holding the*
　　gun in his back. They move to the outside.)

52. DAY. EXT. DUNE COTTAGE
GEORGE, *followed by* DANNY, *walks along the side of the house,*
through the dunes and towards the carriage on the beach.
GEORGE: Would you mind telling me who you are?
DANNY: I'm nobody.
GEORGE: Aye, and that's nothing you've got stuck in my back.
DANNY: I'm a musician.
　　(GEORGE *stops, shocked.* DANNY *hits him in the back and he*
　　falls to the ground.)
　　Don't stop.
GEORGE: I won't, I won't.

(*He gets to his feet and starts to walk towards the sea.*)

DANNY: What's your name?

GEORGE: George.

DANNY: She's very beautiful, George.

GEORGE: Who?

DANNY: On the wall. Your wife?

GEORGE: She's not my wife. She's my sister.

DANNY: I don't remember things, George. I want you to help
me.

(*They come to the sea. There is an abandoned railway carriage
on the beach.*)

GEORGE: I can't go any further.

DANNY: I want you to remember for me.

GEORGE: I can't . . .

(DANNY *hits him in the face with the gun.* GEORGE *falls to his
knees. He crawls and sits with his back to the carriage.* DANNY
crosses and sits beside him.)

I'm bleeding.

DANNY: I'm sorry.

(GEORGE *starts to move.*)

Don't move.

GEORGE: I won't. I promise.

DANNY: Now tell me.

GEORGE: He had been making payments. Protection money. He
was vermin. What do you do with vermin . . .

DANNY: Tell me about her.

GEORGE: I don't know about her. She just appeared.

DANNY: Who shot her?

GEORGE: She reminded me of someone.

DANNY: Did you shoot her?

GEORGE: No.

DANNY: Who did?

GEORGE: Don't ask questions.

(DANNY *looks up in the sky. A plane passes overhead.*
GEORGE *looks up.*)

Hey, what's your name?

(*He looks at* DANNY *through half-closed eyes.*)

That thing doesn't suit ye –
(*He reaches into his pocket for something.* DANNY *shoots.*
GEORGE's *hand comes out holding a white handkerchief. He
has been shot in the neck.* DANNY *rises and moves to*
GEORGE.)

DANNY: You shouldn't have done that – (GEORGE *opens his
mouth to speak, but can't.*)
Tell me, George?

GEORGE: Don't leave me now.

DANNY: George . . . George . . . Tell me, George.

53. DAY. INT. VAN.

BILL *is driving.* DEIRDRE *and* DANNY *sit in the front of the van.*

BILL: Now, we're playing at eight. We can hang around the
camp till then. It's our first gig so make it a good one.
(*He turns the corner. The van comes to a stop – the
photographers click their cameras and flash bulbs.*)
Right. The two of you first.

DEIRDRE: Why?

BILL: Appearances.
(DANNY *takes his dark glasses from his pocket, opens the door
and puts his glasses on. He gets out of the van followed by*
DEIRDRE.)

54. DAY. EXT. HOLIDAY CAMP

DANNY *moves along through the onlookers followed by* DEIRDRE.
She catches him up.

DEIRDRE: What's this all about?

DANNY: He paid them. He paid the cameras.

DEIRDRE: Why?

DANNY: That's what managers do.
(DANNY *moves off.*)

55. DAY. INT. DANCE HALL

DANNY *moves into the hall. There are tangoing couples moving
round, wearing cardboard numbers, in what looks like a competition.
There is a small band on the stage, composed mainly of older men,
playing a tango.* DANNY *walks through the tangoing couples, up to*

30

the bandstand. He stands by the saxophonist, who is playing a repetitive accompaniment and looks up as he plays.

DANNY: Did you know Ben Coyne?

SAXOPHONIST: Who?

DANNY: Ben Coyne. You used to play with him in the Shangri-Las.

SAXOPHONIST: I've played in a lot of bands, kid.

DANNY: So have I ...

(SAXOPHONIST *resumes playing.* DANNY *watches the dancing.* DEIRDRE *is sitting at a table watching him.*)

COMPÈRE: Ladies and Gentlemen, I am sorry to say couples seven and four have been eliminated. But we will continue with a samba.

(*The band go into the samba.*)

DEIRDRE: Should have known you'd be here.

DANNY: Your man's a cowboy. Fancy a samba kid?

DEIRDRE: I fancy you.

(DANNY *and* DEIRDRE *begin dancing.*)

Who taught you to dance?

DANNY: My Auntie Mae.

(*They begin to do extravagant turns.*)

DEIRDRE: We could win this, you know. We could leave them standing.

DANNY: We're too young –

(*The* COMPÈRE *speaks from the bandstand.*)

COMPÈRE: Would all couples not in the competition please leave the floor.

DEIRDRE: He means us.

DANNY: Let's join the competition.

DEIRDRE: You need a number.

COMPÈRE: Clear the floor, please. Please clear the floor.

(*Dancing couples move to the edge of the dance floor. The music stops.* DANNY *and* DEIRDRE *continue dancing, humming the music themselves. They end with a flourish.* DANNY *picks up* DEIRDRE *and carries her off.*)

56. DAY. EXT. SEASCAPE
The band are on the promenade in their new pink show band suits.

DANNY *is fixing his hair.* DEIRDRE *is standing by him.*

BILL: Danny! Di! Come on, we'll never get finished. Come on.
> (*The band moves from the promenade down to the beach. They
> form a line, and a photographer begins taking photos of them.
> They move off.*)

57. NIGHT. INT. DANCE HALL

DEIRDRE *singing 'Danny Boy' – couples dancing.*

58. NIGHT. INT. BAR

DEIRDRE *standing in the bar in front of a neon tree.* DANNY *enters
playing his sax.*

DEIRDRE: See, we make a pair.

DANNY: Why didn't you tell me that before?

DEIRDRE: I didn't notice.

DANNY: Nice tree, isn't it? Want to make a wish?

59. NIGHT. EXT. BEACH

DEIRDRE *and* DANNY *walk along the beach. They stop in front of
a bonfire.* DANNY *takes her arm.*

DANNY: Can I stay with you tonight?

DEIRDRE: Ask my manager.

DANNY: He's dead.
> (DEIRDRE *looks at him, suddenly troubled.*)

DEIRDRE: I didn't mean that.
> (*They turn and move on. Cut to the interior of a chalet bedroom.*)
> What time is it?

DANNY: Twenty past twelve. You a convent girl?

DEIRDRE: I'm a woman, Danny.

DANNY: Tell me what a sin is.

DEIRDRE: It's a habit Catholics indulge in.

DANNY: What about Protestants?

DEIRDRE: (*Takes his dark glasses off*) They don't know what
> sinning is.
> (*She kisses him.*) You do though.
> (*He kisses her back.*)

60. DAWN. INT. CHALET

DEIRDRE *is standing by the window.* DANNY *is asleep.* DEIRDRE

*goes into the bathroom, takes a drink of water then moves back into
the bedroom and sits on the bed.* DANNY *opens his eyes.*

DEIRDRE: You move me, you know that. You never did before.
  (DANNY *places his saxophone neckpiece over her head. They
  kiss.*)

61. DAY. EXT. SEASIDE
The band are travelling back in the van. DEIRDRE *is sitting beside*
DANNY. *The van comes to a stop.* DANNY *gets out.* DEIRDRE
hands him his sax case.

DEIRDRE: You never played your soprano.
DANNY: I'm waiting for the right tune.
  (DANNY *slams the van door.*)
  See you Monday.
  (*The van drives off. There is a Salvation Army band playing.*
  DANNY *moves towards them.*)

62. DAY. EXT. SMALL TOWN BEACH
DANNY *is sitting on the pebbled beach, staring out to sea. Beside
him is the tuba player of the Salvation Army band. He is playing a
mournful tune on the tuba.*

TUBA PLAYER: I've played with them all. The Clipper Carlton,
  The Romantics, Johnny Wyndham and the Blue Lagoon.
  (*He starts to play again.*)
DANNY: And now?
TUBA PLAYER: I play for the Lord.
  (*He continues with his tune.*)

63. NIGHT. INT. MAE'S FLAT
DANNY *enters through front door, carrying cases.* MAE *is listening to
the radio. She moves into the hall.*

MAE: Someone called to see you.
DANNY: Who?
MAE: A government man . . .
  (DANNY *puts down his cases. He takes off his coat.* MAE *moves
  in to help him.*)
  Did you show them?
DANNY: What?

33

MAE: Did you make them dance?

DANNY: They would have done that anyway, Mae.

(DANNY *sits down opposite her.*)

MAE: Listen. Do you remember I taught you to dance?

(*She begins to move her feet to the music from the radio.*)
Come on.

(*They dance.* DANNY *moves his feet in time with hers. They embrace.*)
Oh, Danny!

(MAE *leaves* DANNY *standing alone.*)

64. DAY. INT. CINEMA

DEIRDRE *is playing with the bingo machine in the foyer of the cinema, waiting for* DANNY.

DEIRDRE: Hurry up, Danny.

(DANNY *enters foyer and sees* BONNER *coming through the door.* DEIRDRE *looks up.*

BONNER *moves towards* DANNY. DANNY *moves to* BONNER.)

BONNER: They want you.

(*He moves to the bingo machine and releases the balls. He moves back to* DANNY.)

You'd better come.

(BONNER *exits followed by* DANNY.)

65. DAY. INT. POLICE MORGUE

BONNER *and* DANNY.

DANNY: What is this place?

BONNER: It's a dormitory – it's where people sleep. If you listen you can hear them.

DANNY: Hear what?

BONNER: Sleeping.

(*He opens the door and pulls the* ASSISTANT's *body out. He gets hold of* DANNY's *head and pushes it down to the body. On doing so,* DANNY *hits his head on the side of the door.*

BONNER *removes the plastic cover from the* ASSISTANT's *head.*)

You know him. And you, you know me now.

(BLOOM *enters the room. He moves to the other side of the*

34

body, *signals* BONNER *to leave the room, and confronts*
DANNY. *Both of them look at the body*.)

BLOOM: Maybe he was in love. Were you ever in love, Danny?

DANNY: Yes.

BLOOM: Well, maybe he was too. I would hope he was.
Wouldn't you? Wouldn't you?

DANNY: I would –

BLOOM: What do you know, Danny?

DANNY: Nothing.

BLOOM: Aye, I know nothing too. You've got to watch nothing.
It can take hold of you.
(BLOOM *takes hold of* DANNY's *hands, suddenly gentle*.)
Be careful for those hands, Danny. You need them. Don't
you?

DANNY: I'm a musician.

BLOOM: 'If music be the food of love . . .' How does it go?

DANNY: 'Play on.'

BLOOM: You know, Danny, you can go places I never could.
You understand?

DANNY: I do.

BLOOM: A kind of poetic licence.
(*He looks from* DANNY *to the body*.)
She was very beautiful – when she was like that . . .
(BLOOM *replaces the plastic cover over the face of the*
ASSISTANT.)

66. DAY. INT. VAN

*The band are driving through Portlaoise. The van swings through a
large gate, up a driveway towards a hospital-like building and
draws to a halt.*

DEIRDRE: This is a mental hospital.

BILL: I know. They run a gig here for the locals.

67. DAY. INT. DANCE HALL

Members of the band cross the hall. DANNY *is standing, putting a
reed in his sax.* DEIRDRE *crosses the hall. She stops on seeing*
DANNY.

DEIRDRE: There's tea down the way, if you want some.

35

DANNY: I want to try the sound.

(DEIRDRE *makes to go. Then she turns.*)

DEIRDRE: What's wrong with you, Danny?

DANNY: Nothing.

(DEIRDRE *looks at him for a moment, then goes.*

DANNY begins to play random notes on the sax. He has his eyes closed and plays cascades of notes which seem to echo through the hospital back to him. He opens his eyes as he plays and he sees two or three patients standing down the hall, their backs to the walls, listening to him. They are staring at him without expression. He closes his eyes again and plays on. When he opens them again, the number of patients there has doubled. He keeps his eyes open and watches as they slowly file in round the wall, like ghosts, all of their eyes staring at him, as if willing the music out of him. The notes DANNY is playing seem to express the spirit of each one of them and his eyes slowly assume the same expression as theirs.

A female nurse walks in and claps her hands briskly. The patients slowly file back out again. DANNY stops playing.)

68. DAY. EXT. MENTAL HOSPITAL

DANNY *is standing by a large tree.* DEIRDRE *walks across towards him.*

DEIRDRE: Danny, they want you.

DANNY: Wait a while.

(*He puts a flower in her hair.*)

DEIRDRE: What's with you, Danny?

DANNY: I want to look at you, that's all.

(*He leans over and kisses her.*)

DEIRDRE: You're nuts.

DANNY: Yes. Like them –

(*He turns her round. There are two patients gazing at them.*)

69. NIGHT. INT. HOSPITAL CORRIDOR

Several patients stand around the corridors listening to DEIRDRE's *singing.* DEIRDRE *can be seen singing 'Strange Fruit' to an unseen crowd.*

70. NIGHT. INT. HOTEL BEDROOM

DANNY *finishes brushing his teeth.* DEIRDRE *sits on the bed. He moves towards her. He touches her face. She pushes his hand away.*

DEIRDRE: I can't.

DANNY: Why not?

DEIRDRE: Because you have to tell me first. What is it?

DANNY: It's nothing.

DEIRDRE: You're lying.

DANNY: It's like a nothing you can feel. And it gets worse.

DEIRDRE: You see, you move me. Ever since I met you in that room. With all those flowers. And I wish you didn't.

71. DAY. INT. CAFÉ

DANNY *and* BILL *are drinking coffee.* BILL *finishes his quickly.*

BILL: There's gear to shift. (*He rises and he looks at* DANNY.) Are you listening? There's gear to shift.

DANNY: Let me finish this.

(*As* BILL *goes he passes the waitress. It is the* BRIDE *of the first dance.*)

BRIDE: You're the saxman, aren't you?

DANNY: How do you know?

BRIDE: You asked me to dance once. Don't you remember?
(DANNY *looks at her closely.*)
I was wearing white –

DANNY: You were just married.

BRIDE: Aye, I was. (*She crosses back to the counter with a tray.*)

DANNY: What do you mean, was?

BRIDE: Och, y'know, men. Start out angels, end up brutes. It
began that night.

DANNY: What night?

BRIDE: The night I met you, dumbo. My wedding night. He
vanished, before the dance was over. I didn't see him till
five, the next day.
(DANNY'*s face becomes suddenly alert, as if he is realizing
something.* DANNY *rises and moves to the counter.*)
(*She leans forward.*) Went from bad to worse. I had more
black eyes than pimples.
(*She looks up at him, brightens.*) So how are you, saxman?

Where're you playin'?

DANNY: In Six Mile Bridge. Will you come?

BRIDE: You askin'?

DANNY: I'll leave a pass for you at the door.

BRIDE: I might come –

DANNY: Promise –

BRIDE: Why're you so eager?

DANNY: I remember your eyes.

72. NIGHT. INT. DANCE HALL
The hall is crowded, the band playing. The BRIDE *is standing below the bandstand, looking up at* DANNY.

73. NIGHT. EXT. STAGE DOOR
The BRIDE *is waiting at the stage door.* DANNY *comes out.*

BRIDE: I thought you weren't coming. Where's your car?
   (DANNY *points to the car and moves towards it.*)
   God, you're full of chat.
   (BRIDE *moves away and gets into the car.* DEIRDRE *comes to the stage door and sees* DANNY *and the* BRIDE *driving off.*)

74. NIGHT. EXT. PETROL STATION
They drive into a petrol station. The BRIDE *is beside him. She seems a little nervous.*

BRIDE: You're fast, aren't you? I knew you would be, all you men in bands –

DANNY: Five pounds' worth, please.
   (*He drives off.*)

75. NIGHT. INT. TINY COTTAGE
DANNY *and the* BRIDE *enter the bedroom.*

DANNY: What age is he?

BRIDE: I forget.

DANNY: You couldn't forget.

BRIDE: He'll be thirty-three next Wednesday. Ten years and three months older than me. If you're interested.

DANNY: Will you send him a card?

BRIDE: Maybe we could become penpals.

(DANNY *puts his arms around her and kisses her neck. He starts to unbutton her dress. She moves away from him. He follows.*)
Nobody's touched me, since.
(*They kiss.*)

76. NIGHT. INT. BEDROOM
The BRIDE *and* DANNY *are in bed, the blankets pulled up around them.* DANNY *keeps twisting the dial of a small radio.*
BRIDE: You don't look at all like him –
DANNY: Did he sleep on this side?
   (*He lies beneath the blankets beside her for a moment, very quiet, as if sensing the other.*)
BRIDE: You sound as if you're jealous of him.
   (DANNY *turns to her. He begins to caress her.*)
DANNY: I am. I want to know everything he ever did with you.
BRIDE: Ask away.
DANNY: When he came back to you on your first night, did he – ?
BRIDE: That wasn't my first –
DANNY: But did he – ?
BRIDE: He always wanted it, no matter when he came back. I was so young. I was only twenty-two.
DANNY: Am I like him?
BRIDE: Oh darling –
   (*They kiss.*)
   You're like him now.

77. NIGHT. INT. BEDROOM
Later. DANNY *and the* BRIDE *are lying on the bed.*
BRIDE: He's got a woman, you know. He meets her every lunchtime, up in the forestry where he works . . .

78. DAY. EXT. FOREST
There is a couple sitting on a pile of logs, kissing. DANNY *approaches through the trees. He stops and watches them.*
BETH: What'll we do when it rains?
JOHN: We'll use the hut.

BETH: I don't like it in there.

JOHN: Have you any better ideas?

> (*She picks up her bag. She rises.* JOHN *follows. They move forward and stop.*)

I like you, Beth. You're my soul.

BETH: You're a Prod. They don't have souls.

> (*They walk through the woods, past the hut, and into their car.*)

79. DAY. INT. MOVING CAR

BETH: You take me home.

JOHN: You know me. I'll take you anywhere.

BETH: I know that. That's what I'm worried about.

> (JOHN *is driving fast, along a high winding road through the mountains.* DANNY *appears from the back seat and prods a gun in* JOHN's *neck.*)

DANNY: Keep going.

BETH: Mister, you can let me go. Oh Jesus. Couldn't you just take him? I was going to stop seeing him anyways –

> (JOHN *strikes her violently with the back of his hand. She falls silent.*)

JOHN: It's not me you want, you know. There's someone bigger than me.

> (DANNY *says nothing.*)

I'll take you to him. I'm only small fry. (*He laughs.*) Isn't that right, Beth?

DANNY: How did you do it?

JOHN: Do what?

DANNY: That night. The dance hall.

JOHN: It's not that hard, once you put your mind to it. You know yourself –

DANNY: I do.

> (*He looks in the mirror at* JOHN.)

JOHN: Aye.

> (*He drives the car faster.* DANNY *doesn't seem to notice.*)

You're only a boy. You can't afford to be a boy in our line of business. But he'll tell you himself. He'll tell you it all.

DANNY: Where is he?

JOHN: He's never too far . . .

(*He pushes the car even faster. By now it is careering along tiny roads, with a drop to one side.* BETH *whimpers.*)

(*Laughing*) Aye, I'll take you to him. I'll take you to hell. You believe in hell, don't you?

(BETH *screams.*)

You too, Beth. We'll all go burn together. Y'see me and him, Beth, we know where the badness is, don't we?

DANNY: How did you shoot her?

JOHN: It's easy. You just pull the trigger. Well, go on, you little bugger. Go on. Pull it, pull it. You're gonna shoot me anyway. Pull it. Go on, you little fucker, go on. Pull the trigger. Shoot me, go on, shoot me, shoot me.

(DANNY *shoots.* JOHN *falls over the wheel. The car careers off the road, bursts through a fence and comes to a stop in a field.*)

80. DAY. EXT. FIELD

The car has come to a stop in the field. BETH *is sobbing.* JOHN's *head is shattered. The door is pushed open and* DANNY *crawls out of it. He is bleeding around the forehead. His side is also hurt.*

81. NIGHT. EXT. MARQUEE IN FIELD

There is a large marquee set in a field. DANNY *walks towards it.*

82. NIGHT. INT. MARQUEE

DANNY *walks through a flap into the marquee. On the stage, he sees* BILL *with a man in an anorak. He is holding a wad of notes.*

BILL: Tell your boss, thanks a lot. I feel extremely protected. Now there's £135 there.

MAN: OK. OK.

(*He sees* DANNY *approaching.*)

Get him out of here.

(DANNY *walks towards the* MAN. *He grips him by the shoulders.*)

DANNY: Give it back to him.

MAN: Now hold on, kid –

DANNY: (*Screaming*) Give it to him –

(*The* MAN *hesitates once more.* DANNY *shoots him in the chest. The* MAN *staggers back.* DANNY *shoots him a second time.*

42

He takes the wad of notes from the MAN's *hands. He goes to*
BILL *who is speechless.*)
That's why they did it to Ray, Bill.
(BILL *doesn't move to take the proffered notes.* DANNY *stuffs
them into* BILL's *top pocket.*)
He was making payments.
(DEIRDRE *is standing by the entrance. She looks stunned by
what she sees.*)
DEIRDRE: (*In a whisper*) Is this what you couldn't tell me –
DANNY: Di –
(*He reaches out to touch her. The gun brushes off her arm. She
screams.*)
DEIRDRE: Don't touch me – you're dead. You're rotten –
(*He holds her. She struggles with him, hitting him around the
head and shoulders, crying.*)
Fuck you, Danny. Fuck you blind –
(*She slowly calms down.* DANNY *holds her lightly with the gun
in one hand.*)
You make me feel ... unclean ...
(DANNY *lets go of her. He walks slowly away. She looks at him.*)
They were looking for you –
DANNY: Who?
DEIRDRE: (*Screaming again*) Them – like you – only in uniform.
(DANNY *retreats into the darkness.* DEIRDRE *moves to the door
and looks after him, then walks around the body and up on to
the stage to* BILL.)

83. NIGHT. EXT. SEA
DANNY *walks along the seashore away from the marquee.*

84. DAY. EXT. FARMHOUSE
DANNY *approaches the farmhouse. He walks under the arch. He
looks and sees a tall, middle-aged woman at the washing line.*
DANNY *approaches her. She turns towards him.*
MARY: What do you want?
DANNY: Clothes. Have you got a husband?
(MARY *nods.*)
What's your name?

43

MARY: Mary.
DANNY: Would you show me his clothes, Mary?
  (*She shakes her head.*)
  I have a gun.
  (*They move into the house.*)

85. DAY. INT. BEDROOM
DANNY *is putting on her husband's clothes.* MARY *has a pair of trousers in her hand. She crosses to him and hands him the trousers. He puts them on.*
DANNY: Does he fit me?
MARY: Better than he fits himself.
DANNY: Do you love him, Mary?
  (*She looks at him with terrified eyes and shakes her head.*)
  Will you cut my hair?
  (*He picks up his gun and sits in the chair. She crosses to the fireplace, picks up the scissors and turns.*)

86. DAY. INT. BEDROOM
DANNY *is sitting in his new clothes with his gun in his lap.* MARY *is cutting his hair.*
MARY: You don't want them to know you? Whoever they are?
DANNY: No.
MARY: It's very short.
DANNY: Good.
MARY: I've a mind it won't suit you. He always wore it short.
DANNY: Where is he?
MARY: He's dead.
  (*She clips one side of his head very short.*)
  I've better scissors downstairs.
  (*She goes down.* DANNY *sits there for a long time. Then he stands up and looks around.*)
DANNY: Mary?
  (*There is no reply. He goes out of the room.*)

87. DAY. INT. KITCHEN
DANNY: (*Moves into the kitchen through the doorway*) Mary.
  (*He sees* MARY *standing at an open drawer. He crosses to her.*)

44

Mary.
(MARY *turns and stabs him in the hand with a large knife. He
hits her on the side of the head with his gun. She falls to the
floor, dropping the knife.*)
You shouldn't have done that.
(DANNY *turns and takes a tea cloth from the wall. He binds his
hand. He picks up the scissors.*)
You have to finish my hair.
(*He turns and exits from the kitchen.*)

88. DAY. INT. BEDROOM
DANNY *walks to the mirror and starts to cut the rest of his hair.*

89. DAY. INT. KITCHEN
MARY *is seated by the side of the chest of drawers.* DANNY *walks
into the room carrying his gun. He stops and looks down at her.*
DANNY: Have you any food?
    (MARY *sits silently rubbing the side of her head. He turns and
    exits from the kitchen.*)

90. DAY. EXT. FARMYARD

He walks into a small farm building – hens fly in all directions – he takes out some eggs and returns to the kitchen.

91. DAY. INT. KITCHEN

MARY *is sitting by the table.* DANNY *has cooked some eggs. He ladles them on to a plate in front of her.*

DANNY: Eat it.

> (*She begins to eat, obediently.*)

92. NIGHT. INT. HIS BEDROOM

DANNY *is lying on the bed, propped against the pillows.* MARY *is bandaging* DANNY's *hand.*

DANNY: Was he a good man?

MARY: He was.

DANNY: Why don't you have a sleep?

> (MARY *shakes her head. She stands by the dressing table, then starts to wander around the room.*)

MARY: That gun. Who taught you to use it?

DANNY: Him that I'm after.

MARY: You know him then? He's a friend of yours?

DANNY: He's an acquaintance.

MARY: Why do you want him?

DANNY: I don't know any more.

MARY: It's not me needs a sleep. It's you.

> (DANNY's *head falls on his chest. His eyes close.*)
> Hating is easy, that's what I found out. It has its own ways. It just grows. My man whose clothes you're in. I hated him for years. I'd stand beside him at mass and pray: 'Lord, let me be free of him.' Love is kind, the priest told me. But I never felt it. Then he went. I felt ... Will I tell you what I felt?
> (*She looks at the luminous eyes in the picture of Christ above the bed.*)
> Wherever you stand, his eyes stare right at you.
> (*She leans over and takes the gun from his lap. We see his sleeping face. A click is heard.* DANNY'S *eyes open.*)

I'll show you what I felt.
(DANNY *sits up in horror.*)
DANNY: No!
(*There is the sound of the gun exploding.* MARY *slides down the wall, having shot herself in the head, the gun in her hand.*)

93. DAWN. EXT. FARMYARD
DANNY *runs across the farmyard to the van. He opens the door and sits at the wheel. There is a chicken there, which flies around, squawking. He grabs it with his hands and throws it out of the window. He drives away.*

94. DAY. EXT. FIELDS
DANNY *drives the van across the open countryside. It jams on a rock. He gets out and collapses in despair on the bonnet of the van.*

95. DAY. EXT. FIELDS
DANNY *walks across the bogland. He approaches the burnt-out dance hall.*

47

96. DAY. EXT. FIELDS

DANNY *walks on to the tarmac. There is a silver caravan. There is a* MAN *standing outside it.* DANNY *walks towards him. A queue has formed outside the caravan.*

DANNY *stares at the* MAN. *The* MAN *walks along the queue.*

MAN: Young Francie Thompson. Seventh son of a seventh son. Two pounds a sitting.

(DANNY *walks inside the caravan.*)

97. DAY. INT. CARAVAN

At one end of the caravan, a boy, FRANCIE, *stands with a woman kneeling in front of him. He touches her neck with water from a bowl beside him. He looks up and sees* DANNY *standing at the end of the caravan.*

FRANCIE: You'll have to wait your turn.

(*To the woman*) May God and his holy Mother bless you, ma'am.

(*The woman exits.* FRANCIE *beckons* DANNY *to him.*

DANNY *moves forward to* FRANCIE.)
What ails you, sir?
DANNY: Have you really got the power?
    (FRANCIE *touches* DANNY'*s hand.*)
FRANCIE: I have.
DANNY: Where are you from, kid?
FRANCIE: Derry City.
DANNY: Where did you get the suit?
FRANCIE: My uncle bought it.
    (DANNY *faints. The boy looks down at him. The* MAN *arrives through the door.*
MAN: Leave him be, Francie.
    (BONNER *enters the caravan just as* DANNY *rises.*)
BONNER: Half the country's looking for you. You've been a bad
    boy.
    (*He takes hold of* DANNY *and they exit from the caravan. Young* FRANCIE *watches.*)

98. DAY. EXT. CARAVAN
BONNER *takes hold of* DANNY *by the back of the neck and they move towards the derelict ballroom.*
BONNER: A bad, bad boy.

99. DAY. INT. BALLROOM
BONNER: Here we are again. 'Vengeance is mine.' Who said
    that?
DANNY: I don't know.
BONNER: The Lord said that.
    (*He throws* DANNY *away from him further into the dance hall.* DANNY *backs away.* BONNER *takes out a gun and cocks it. He advances towards* DANNY.)
DANNY: Where's Bloom?
BONNER: He's late again. It's a lot easier to play than a
    saxophone.
DANNY: It is.
BONNER: And always the same tune . . .
DANNY: What's your name?
BONNER: Thomas.

(FRANCIE *enters from the open side of the dance hall and moves towards them.*)

Here's a boy believes in miracles. Do you?

DANNY: I do.

(*A shot is fired –* BONNER *staggers.* DANNY *moves forward.* BONNER *clings to him.*)

BONNER: Stay with me.

DANNY: I can't.

BONNER: I grew up round here.

DANNY: So did she.

(DANNY *moves to the door.* BLOOM *is standing there holding a gun.*)

Why didn't you tell me, Mr Bloom?

BLOOM: I didn't know.

DANNY: You wanted me to find out –

(BLOOM *turns and moves out of the burnt-out ballroom, followed by* DANNY *and* FRANCIE. *The wind blows posters and dust outside the ballroom.*)